FROGGY'S FIRST KISS

FROGGY'S FIRST KISS

by JONATHAN LONDON
illustrated by FRANK REMKIEWICZ

PUFFIN BOOKS

For Aaron & Sean, two Froggies,
and for their mother, Maureen

And for a very special librarian, Marilynne McLaughlin
—J.L.

For the Valentines: Ken, Alma, and Rhapsody
—F.R.

PUFFIN BOOKS
Published by the Penguin Group
Penguin Putnam Books for Young Readers, 345 Hudson Street, New York, New York 10014, U.S.A.
Penguin Books Ltd, 27 Wrights Lane, London W8 5TZ, England
Penguin Books Australia Ltd, Ringwood, Victoria, Australia
Penguin Books Canada Ltd, 10 Alcorn Avenue, Toronto, Ontario, Canada M4V 3B2
Penguin Books (N.Z.) Ltd, 182-190 Wairau Road, Auckland 10, New Zealand

Penguin Books Ltd, Registered Offices: Harmondsworth, Middlesex, England

First published in the United States of America by Viking, a member of Penguin Putnam Inc., 1998
Published by Puffin Books, a member of Penguin Putnam Books for Young Readers, 2000

10 9 8 7 6 5 4

Text copyright © Jonathan London, 1998
Illustrations copyright © Frank Remkiewicz, 1998
All rights reserved

THE LIBRARY OF CONGRESS HAS CATALOGED THE VIKING EDITION AS FOLLOWS:
London, Jonathan.
Froggy's first kiss / by Jonathan London ; illustrated by Frank Remkiewicz. p. cm.
Summary: As Valentine's Day approaches, Froggy thinks that he is falling in love with
the new girl in class, but his feelings change when she gives him their first kiss.
ISBN 0-670-87064-1
[1. Valentine's Day—Fiction. 2. Frogs—Fiction. 3. Schools—Fiction.] I. Remkiewicz, Frank, ill. II. Title.
PZ7.L8432Fu 1998 [E]—dc21 97-18772 CIP AC

Puffin Books ISBN 0-14-056570-1

Printed in the United States of America

It was the week before Valentine's Day,
and for Froggy,
Valentine's Day meant candy.
But it also meant love.

At school, Froggy's mind wandered.

FRROGGYY!

cried his teacher,
Miss Witherspoon.

"Wha-a-a-a-t?"
"Kindly pay attention, dear."

And that's when he saw
the prettiest girl frog
in the world:
the new girl in class.

Her name was Frogilina,
and when she smiled at him

his insides got all
soft and wiggly,
like he'd had caterpillars
for breakfast.

FRRROOGGYY!

called his teacher.

"Wha-a-a-a-t?"
"Your eyes should be on your work, dear.
It's not polite to stare."
"Oops," said Froggy.

At recess, Frogilina smiled at him
through the monkey bars.
He was hanging upside down . . .

and when he saw her
he fell smack on his head—*bonk!*

At lunch, Frogilina sat beside him.
She smiled and opened her lunch box.
"I have a treat for you, Froggy.
Close your eyes."

And she gave
him a big juicy apple.

After lunch, Froggy and Frogilina
played tetherball together.
Frogilina wound up, socked the ball . . .

and Froggy was so busy gazing into her eyes . . .
the ball hit him in the head—*bonk!*—
and knocked him down.

At lunch the next day,
Frogilina smiled and opened her lunch box.
"I have a goody for you, Froggy.
Close your eyes."

And she gave him a cookie
shaped like a heart.

That afternoon, Froggy and his class
made valentines. They cut hearts
out of paper. Some big . . .
some little . . .
some red . . .
some pink.

And on just one, Froggy wrote, I LOVE YOU.
He didn't want any of his classmates to see—
especially Frogilina—
so he worked under his desk.

called Miss Witherspoon.

When Froggy stood up,
he hit his head on his desk—*bonk!*—
and everybody laughed.
Especially Frogilina.

At lunch the next day, Frogilina sat beside him again.
She smiled and opened her lunch box.
"I have a surprise for you, Froggy.
Close your eyes."
And what do you think she gave him?

A big juicy . . . **KISS!**
Smack on his cheek!

Froggy grabbed his lunch box
and flopped away—*flop flop flop*.

His tummy felt so weird
he couldn't eat his lunch.
Not even dessert.

On the bus home after school,
everybody teased him—
even Max, his best friend.
They sang: "*Froggy has a girlfriend!
Froggy has a girlfriend!*"

"No I *don't!*"
cried Froggy.

When the bus stopped
he flopped all the way home—
flop flop flop.

But his heart
felt heavy.
Was it love?
Was it hunger?
Was it his backpack
filled with valentine cards?

"What did you do at school today, Froggy?"
asked his mother.
"We made valentines," said Froggy.

"Did you make one for someone . . . *special?*"
Froggy turned almost purple
and flopped into his room—*flop flop flop.*

But the next morning, on Valentine's Day,
Froggy served his mother
breakfast in bed, and said,
"Mom, that someone special . . .
is *you!*"

And he gave his mother the big heart with the I LOVE YOU.

And his mother gave Froggy
a whole *bunch* of kisses.
Candy kisses!